AD SOLEM

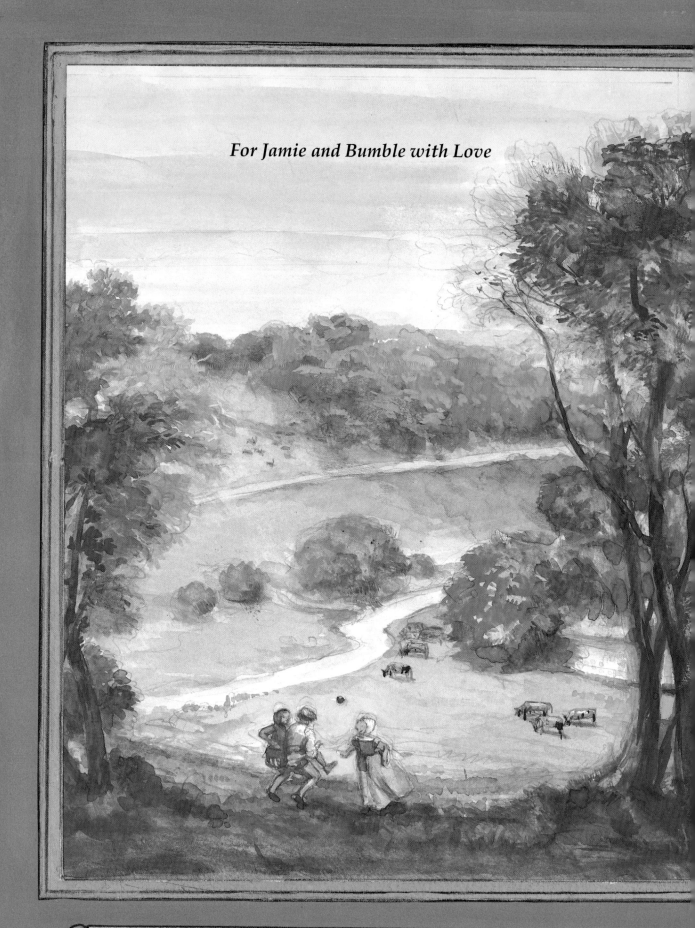

For Jamie and Bumble with Love

 Maxwell Macmillan International
New York   Oxford   Singapore   Sydney

John S. Goodall

GREAT DAYS OF A
COUNTRY
HOUSE

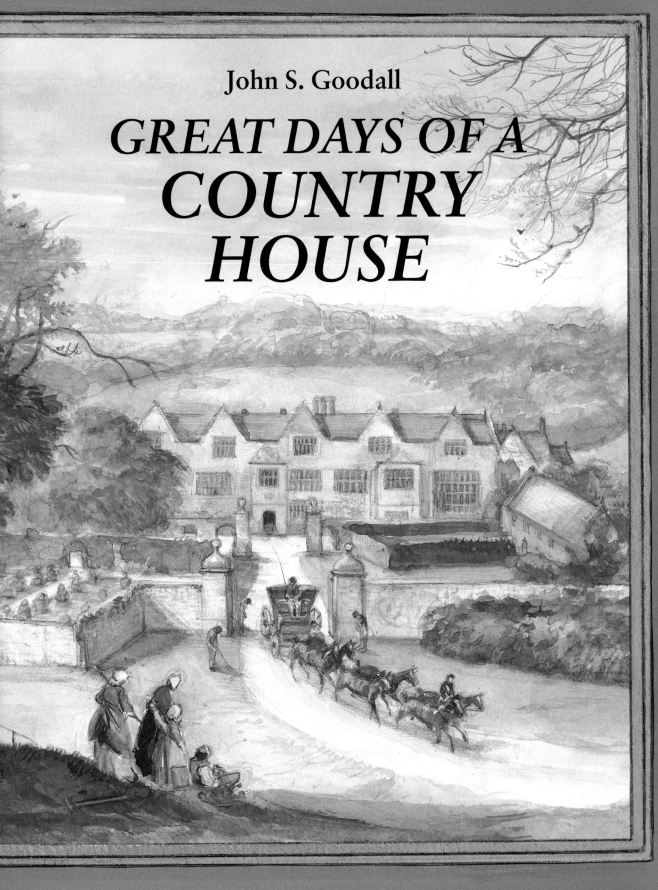

MARGARET K. MCELDERRY BOOKS
New York

TUDOR PERIOD
1485 – 1603

The owners of the house welcome their guests

TUDOR PERIOD
1485 – 1603

A great feast with music and entertainment

*Above stairs, a dinner party served by footmen
means hard work below stairs*

 LATE GEORGIAN PERIOD
1760 – 1810

*Churning, washing, polishing and preparing a meal
are all part of the day's work*

 LATE GEORGIAN PERIOD
1760 – 1810

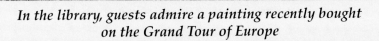

*In the library, guests admire a painting recently bought
on the Grand Tour of Europe*

REGENCY PERIOD
1810 – 1830

An evening spent playing the fashionable card game of bezique

 REGENCY PERIOD
1810 – 1830

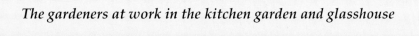
The gardeners at work in the kitchen garden and glasshouse

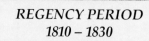

REGENCY PERIOD
1810 – 1830

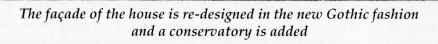

*The façade of the house is re-designed in the new Gothic fashion
and a conservatory is added*

The nursery, with a hot bath ready for the children

VICTORIAN PERIOD
1837 – 1901

A dinner party to celebrate New Year's Eve

 VICTORIAN PERIOD
1837 – 1901

A Christmas party, with games for the children

VICTORIAN PERIOD
1837 – 1901

After dinner the men relax with brandy and a game of billiards

 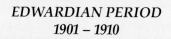

EDWARDIAN PERIOD
1901 – 1910

A visiting soprano entertains the guests at a soirée

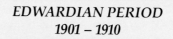

EDWARDIAN PERIOD
1901 – 1910

Afternoon tea and a game of croquet on the lawn

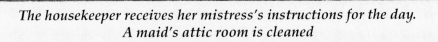

The housekeeper receives her mistress's instructions for the day.
A maid's attic room is cleaned

 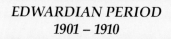

EDWARDIAN PERIOD
1901 – 1910

*Friends gathered for the local hunt's Boxing Day Meet
admire some early cars*

EDWARDIAN PERIOD
1901 – 1910

Elegantly attired, young and old dance the night away

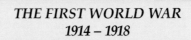

THE FIRST WORLD WAR
1914 – 1918

The house is commandeered for use as a military hospital

THE 1920s

 A tennis party to inaugurate the new grass court

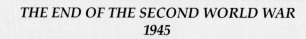

THE END OF THE SECOND WORLD WAR
1945

Run down by wartime use, the house and grounds are in a shabby state